DON'T TELL ME A GHOST STORY

DON'T TELL ME
A GHOST STORY

by Phyllis Rose Eisenberg

Illustrated by Lynn Munsinger

HARCOURT BRACE JOVANOVICH, PUBLISHERS   NEW YORK AND LONDON

*With love
to Manny and Bart
who never say,
"Don't tell me a story."*

Requests for permission to make copies of
any part of the work should be mailed to:
Permissions, Harcourt Brace Jovanovich, Publishers,
757 Third Avenue, New York, New York 10017.

Library of Congress Cataloging in Publication Data
Eisenberg, Phyllis Rose.   Don't tell me a ghost story.
  Summary: An older brother tells a scary ghost story
to his younger brother, only to have the tables turned
on him. [1. Ghosts—Fiction. 2. Brothers and sisters—
Fiction]   I. Munsinger, Lynn, ill.   II. Title.
PZ7.E3463Do   [E]   81-20082
ISBN 0-15-224029-2   AACR2
B C D E   FIRST EDITION

DON'T TELL ME A GHOST STORY

3707

"I'm going to tell you a brand-new ghost story," said Jeff. "*Once upon a—*"

"Don't tell me a ghost story!" said Randy. "They make my skin crawly!"

"But that's how ghost stories are," said Jeff. "*Once upon a time there was an ugly, spooooooky ghost. It had ooooozy eyes and a nose made of moldy beans.*"

"See?" said Randy, putting his fingers into his ears. "I'm not even listening!"

"*And it smelled like sixty sour sausages,*" said Jeff.

"I'v-e b-e-e-n w-o-r-k-i-n-g o-n t-h-e r-a-i-l-r-o-a-d," sang Randy, "a-l-l t-h-e l-i-v-e-l-o-n-g d-a-y!!!"

"*And there was poisoned onion soup sloshing around in its ears.*"

"Singing people can't even *hear* talking people," said Randy. "Tra la la de la!!!"

"*The ghost lived in a house exactly like ours . . . with two brothers exactly like us.*"

"I told you, Jeff, I'm *not* in the mood for a ghost story!"

"One rainy, dark, thundery night, the brothers heard the ghost creeeeeeping down the hall. It was heading for their bedroom! Now the older brother didn't mind at all. But the younger brother minded a lot. His skin got so crawly, it started crumbling up."

"I'm more in the mood for cards," said Randy softly. "Want to play cards?"

"Nope. I'm telling this ghost story if it takes all night. So you'd better listen!"

"I *won't* listen," said Randy. And he put his head under the covers.

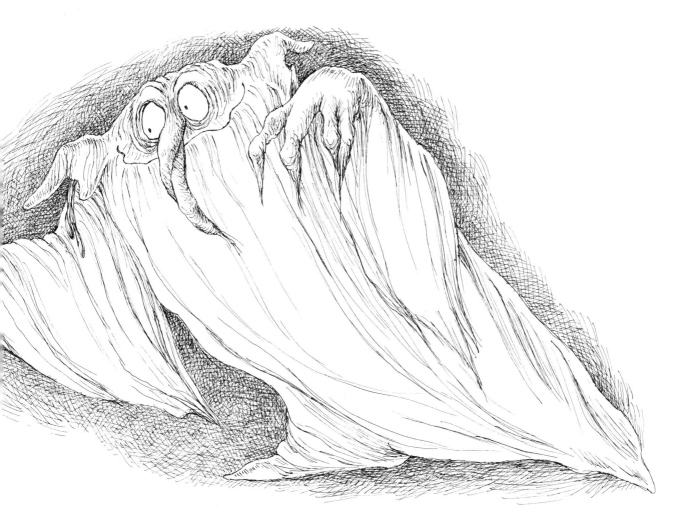

"*So the younger brother put his head under the covers, but that didn't stop the ghost,*" said Jeff. "*It came closer...*" Jeff tiptoed across the room. "*And closer...*" He crept behind Randy's bed and shook it. "*And closer!!!*"

"I—I know that's you, Jeff. So—so cut it out and let's play cards!"

"*Suddenly there was a weird, weird sound: woooooo-eeeeee . . . woooooo-eeeeee!*"

"Have you—have you seen the cards? Maybe I'll . . . play solitaire. . . ."

"You'll never guess who was making the 'woooooo-eeeeee' sound," said Jeff.

"I don't *want* to guess!"

"It was the ghost's uncle, that's who. And after the 'woooooo-eeeeee' he called, '*Mooooooky Bloooooooky, when you're throoooogh haunting, bring me some bluuuuuueberries. I think they're under the rat bones in Dead Skunk Cave.*'

" '*Okay, Uncle dear,*' said the ghost. '*Will do.*'

"*And the uncle ghost said, 'Thanks, Moooooooky Bloooooooky.*' "

"Wait a minute!" said Randy. "What's 'Mooky Blooky'?"

"That's the ghost's name," said Jeff.

"Mooky Blooky? What a dumb name for a ghost!"

"You're saying it wrong," said Jeff. "It's Moooooooky Blooooooky! *So Moooooooky Blooooooky went to Dead Skunk Cave to check out the blueberries. But just when he got to the last rat bone, he saw a gigantic shadow. It belonged to . . . a killer shark!*"

"A shark? You're crazy!" said Randy. "Sharks don't live in caves!"

"Well, this cave was . . . divided down the middle. Half was land. Half was water."

"Oh."

"*So this killer shark was drooling.
It wanted Mooooooky Blooooooky
for dinner. Now Mooooooky Blooooooky
was a brave ghost, but his flesh turned
into 90,000 icicles.*"

"If . . . if I was telling
it," said Randy softly,
"I'd—I'd name the ghost
Marvin . . . or something
like that."

"Well, you're *not* telling it! *It took 32 weeks for Moooooooky Bloooooooky to thaw out. But just when he did, the killer shark's best friend appeared. It was a slobbery, hideous creature, and its favorite hobby was coiling around younger brothers' throats.*"

"Yes," said Randy, his eyes growing wide, "I would definitely call the ghost Marvin."

"Marvin is *not* a scary name."

"My Marvin would have a . . . a very scary cackle."

"Only witches cackle, dopey," said Jeff. "And witches don't belong in ghost stories. Now stop interrupting me!"

"Marvin likes cackling: 'Hee hee heh—heh heh heeeeee!'
And after he cackles, he gets on his broomstick!"

"You are really, really stupid!" said Jeff. "Broomsticks are
for witches, *not* ghosts!"

"Marvin loves broomsticks. He even collects them," said Randy. "*So once upon a time Marvin flew over the older brother's bed. Now the older brother always said he didn't mind ghosts. But he sure minded Marvin because Marvin was the spookiest ghost on the whole block.... He even breathed fire!*"

"You are the world's rottenest ghost storyteller!" said Jeff. "*Dragons* breathe fire—don't you know anything?"

"Well... Marvin's aunt was a dragon," said Randy, "so she showed him how.

"*Now fire-breathing made the big brother very, very nervous, so he said to Marvin, 'I think you've got the wrong house!' But Marvin said, 'It's the right house and also the right brother.' Then he started fire-breathing down the older brother's neck. The older brother hated it because it reminded him of last summer when his back got sunburned and all the blisters popped.*"

"Remember when I told you I could stand on my head... for days?" asked Jeff, getting out of bed.

"*Now the older brother was a mess,*" continued Randy. "*All of his teeth shook. Even his back molars. 'I'm going to haunt you, older brother,' said Marvin, 'until your chin turns to slime.'*"

"Well, when I say something," said Jeff, "I *mean* it!" And Jeff stood on his head right next to Randy's bed. "Look at *this*, Randy! Pretty neat, huh?"

But Randy wouldn't look. He just went on with his story:
"*The older brother said, 'Please don't haunt me, Marvin! I've got to get up for school tomorrow.'*"

"Tomorrow's Saturday," said Jeff. "Ha ha!"

"*'Who cares?' said Marvin. 'Your chin is sliming already!'*"

"It's *not*!" said Jeff.

"It is!" said Randy. "Marvin said it is!"

Jeff touched his chin again and again. Finally he turned on the light and looked in the mirror.

"Hey!" said Randy. "No lights during a ghost story!"

"I just wanted to check my, uh...loose tooth...."

"No lights!" insisted Randy. "*Well, suddenly Marvin took a big box out of his pocket—*"

"Ghosts don't have pockets," said Jeff, standing on his head again.

"Guess what was inside?"

"What?"

"A hungry, ugly monster, with a slushy, mushy mouth," said Randy.

"Monsters don't belong in ghost stories!"

"They do," said Randy. "*So the monster said, 'Please, Marvin, feed me a juicy brother!'*

"*And the monster said, 'Brothers who stand on their heads are* always *juicy!'*"

3707

Jeff scurried into bed.

"No fair, Jeff!" called Randy. "You said you could stand there for days!"

"My feet got cold."

"Oh... *so Marvin said, 'Sorry, Monster. The only juicy brother around here just dried up.'*

"*And the monster said, 'I'll wait until he gets juicy again.'*"

Jeff scooted out of bed and crawled underneath it.

"Now what?" said Randy.

"Listen, Randy . . . tell this Marvin to tell the monster not to wait around."

"It's no use, Jeff. The monster wants to wait."

"Then tell Marvin to tell the monster that the only way

dried-up brothers get juicy again is by staying under their beds . . . until their ninety-eighth birthday."

"Okay," Randy finally said. "I told Marvin. And he said that the monster said that that was a little too long to wait. So—so the monster left, I think."

"What do you mean, 'You think'?"

"Well, you never know with monsters. . . . Listen, Jeff, do you hear that skrish-sh-sh skrosh-sh-sh sound?"

"Yeah. It's coming from the kitchen. . . . Maybe it's Peewee."

"It can't be Peewee!" said Randy. "She's busy . . . guarding the house."

"Peewee? Guarding the house? That's a laugh! She's too little for guarding—or for *anything*! . . . Do you think that maybe it's Moooooooky Bloooooooky's uncle . . . looking for blueberries?"

"Are you kidding?"

"Of course, I'm kidding," said Jeff, forcing a little laugh.

"You're not kidding. I can tell. See? I told you not to tell me a ghost story!" said Randy. "Now you're even afraid of a ghost's relative!"

"I'm not afraid!"

"No? Then why don't you go and look?"

"Okay," said Jeff.

"You mean you're really going?"

"Sure."

"...when?"

Slowly, very slowly, Jeff started down the hall. In a while he was back.

"Well," said Randy, "what was it?"

"The funniest thing happened," said Jeff. "I just happened to stop in the bathroom and guess what—I found the cards! I know how you love to play cards, so I came straight back. Shall I deal?"

"*I'll* deal," said Randy. "And next time I'm telling *my* ghost story first. It'll be about Marvin's other aunt who's a zombie.

And she teaches Marvin how to zom. *So Marvin—*"

"I thought you wanted to play cards," said Jeff.

"*So Marvin zoms the older brother and—*"

"There's no such thing as zom, Randy! Let's play cards!"

"*The older brother felt something squishing in his hair. It was a whole gang of worms. He almost fainted!*"

"Zoms don't belong in ghost stories!" shouted Jeff. "Now do you want to play cards...or...shall I tell you about the six starving vampires? Five wanted Younger Brother Pizza. One wanted Older Brother Rhubarb. As usual, the majority ruled."

"Listen, Jeff, I've been thinking. Since you went to all that trouble getting the cards, maybe we should play..."

"How about Fish?"

"I don't know," said Randy. "Fish sort of reminds me of killer sharks. And they remind me of creatures. And they remind me of..."

"Just deal and stop worrying. Hey! Cut that out!"

"It isn't me!"

"You're—you're not sh-shaking the bed?" whispered Jeff.
"No. I thought it was *you*!"
"It's not me."
"Then who is it?" whispered Randy.

"It's . . . Peewee! Hi, Peewee!!! You're the right size after all!" said Jeff as he and Randy both gave the dog a big hug.

"She likes to be here with us," said Randy.

"I know. Maybe next time we tell ghost stories," said Jeff, "we can let her listen."

"Good idea!" said Randy. "When's next time?"

"How about in ten thousand years?"

"Yeah. That sounds perfect."